RAINBOW magic

SPECIAL EDITION

HOLLY
THE CHRISTMAS FAIRY

By Daisy Meadows

Illustrated by Georgie Ripper

Silver Dolphin

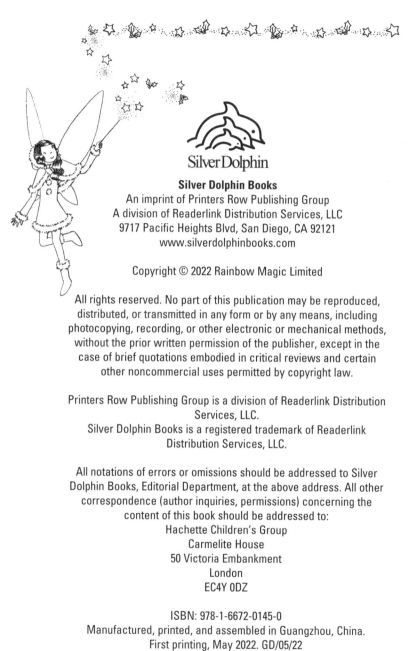

Silver Dolphin Books

An imprint of Printers Row Publishing Group
A division of Readerlink Distribution Services, LLC
9717 Pacific Heights Blvd, San Diego, CA 92121
www.silverdolphinbooks.com

Printers Row Publishing Group is a division of Readerlink Distribution Services, LLC.
Silver Dolphin Books is a registered trademark of Readerlink Distribution Services, LLC.

All notations of errors or omissions should be addressed to Silver Dolphin Books, Editorial Department, at the above address. All other correspondence (author inquiries, permissions) concerning the content of this book should be addressed to:
Hachette Children's Group
Carmelite House
50 Victoria Embankment
London
EC4Y 0DZ

ISBN: 978-1-6672-0145-0
Manufactured, printed, and assembled in Guangzhou, China.
First printing, May 2022. GD/05/22
26 25 24 23 22   1 2 3 4 5

Table of Contents

The Fairyland Palace

Hillfield's Farm

Christmas Trees

HILLFIELD'S FARM

Tippington Town

Jack Frost's
Ice Castle

Santa's
Cabin

RAINBOW SHOPPING CENTER

Rachel's
House

Shopping Center

CHRISTMAS PLANS MAY GO AWRY,
IF I CAN MAKE THESE REINDEER FLY.
SANTA'S GIFTS FOR GIRLS AND BOYS
WILL ALL BECOME MY FUN, NEW TOYS!

MAGIC REINDEER LISTEN WELL
AS I BIND YOU WITH THIS SPELL.
HEAR MY ORDERS, FLY THIS SLEIGH
THROUGH STARRY SKIES AND FAR AWAY.

Find the hidden letters in holly leaves
throughout the book. Unscramble all
nine letters to make a special holiday
word! See page 165 for the answer.

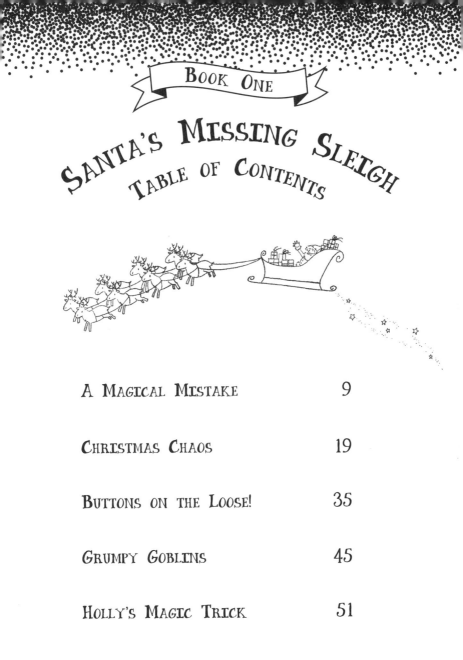

BOOK ONE

SANTA'S MISSING SLEIGH
TABLE OF CONTENTS

A Magical Mistake

"Only three days to go!" Rachel Walker said, sighing happily. She was attaching Christmas cards to long pieces of red ribbon, so that she could hang them on the living room wall. "I love Christmas! Don't you, Kirsty?"

Kirsty Tate, Rachel's best friend, nodded.

"Of course," she replied, handing Rachel another pile of cards. "It's a magical time of year!"

Rachel and Kirsty laughed and touched the golden lockets they both wore around their necks. The two girls shared a wonderful secret. No one else knew it, but they were friends with fairies!

Kirsty and Rachel had visited Fairyland when their fairy friends needed help. They had rescued the Rainbow Fairies after they were cast out of Fairyland by nasty Jack Frost.

In return for their help rescuing the fairies, the Fairy King and Queen had given Rachel and Kirsty each a gold locket. The lockets were full of magical fairy dust. The girls could use it to take them to Fairyland whenever they needed help from the fairies.

"Thanks for asking me to stay," said Kirsty, cutting another piece of ribbon. "Mom says she and Dad will pick me up on Christmas Eve."

"We might get some snow before then!" Rachel said, smiling. "The weather's getting much colder. I wonder what Christmas is like in Fairyland."

Just then, the door opened and Mrs. Walker came into the room. She was followed by Buttons, Rachel's friendly, shaggy dog. He was white with gray patches and a long, furry tail.

"Oh, girls, that looks great!" Rachel's mom exclaimed when she saw the cards hanging on the walls. "We'll go over to Hillfield's Farm and pick out a Christmas tree tonight."

"Hooray!" Rachel cried. "Can Kirsty and I decorate it?"

"We were hoping you would!" Mrs. Walker laughed. "You can get the decorations out of the garage after lunch."

"Buttons seems to love Christmas too," Kirsty said, smiling. The dog was sniffing the cards and ribbons.

"He does," Rachel replied. "Every year, I buy him some doggie treats and wrap them up. And every year, he finds them and eats them before Christmas!"

Buttons wagged his tail. Then he grabbed the end of a ribbon in his mouth, and ran off, trailing red ribbon behind him.

"Buttons, no!" Rachel yelled. She and Kirsty ran after him to get the ribbon back.

When the girls had finished hanging the Christmas cards, they had some hot soup for lunch. Then Rachel took Kirsty out to the garage to find the boxes of decorations.

"It's getting colder," Kirsty said, shivering. "Maybe it will snow!"

"I hope so," Rachel replied. She switched on the garage light. "The decorations are up there." She pointed at a shelf above the workbench. "I'll stand on the stepladder and hand the boxes down to you."

"OK," Kirsty agreed.

Rachel climbed up the ladder and began to pass the boxes down. They were full of silver stars, shiny tinsel, and glittering ornaments in pink, purple, and silver.

"I hope you have a fairy for the top of the tree!" Kirsty joked as Rachel handed her a box.

"No, we don't!" Rachel laughed. "We've always had a silver star, but it's getting old now. Be careful, Kirsty," she continued, lifting another box off the shelf. "This one has all sorts of things sticking out of it. Oh!" Rachel gasped in surprise. The gold locket around her neck had caught on a tiny, sparkling wreath made of twigs. The locket burst open, scattering both girls with fairy dust.

"Oh, no!" Rachel cried, scrambling down from the ladder.

"What should we do?" Kirsty began.

But they didn't have time to do anything. Suddenly, both girls were caught up in a swirling cloud of fairy dust that swept them off their feet. The sparkles whirled around them, glittering in the pale winter light.

"Kirsty, we're shrinking!" Rachel cried. "I think we're on our way to Fairyland!"

CHRISTMAS CHAOS

The girls weren't scared. This had happened to them before! But as they whirled through the clouds toward Fairyland, Rachel felt a bit embarrassed. She hadn't meant to use her magic fairy dust at all—it was an accident!

"Don't worry," called Kirsty, noticing the look on Rachel's face. "It'll be great to see our fairy friends again."

Soon the girls
spotted the
red-and-white
toadstool houses
of Fairyland
below, and then
the silver palace
with its four
pink towers.

As Rachel and
Kirsty drifted
closer to the
palace, they
could see a
crowd of fairies
waving at them.
There was King
Oberon and
Queen Titania

with the Rainbow Fairies too. "Hello!" called Ruby and Sunny. As the girls landed on the ground, the fairies crowded around them. Rachel quickly tried to explain. "I'm sorry," she gasped. "We didn't mean to come. It was an accident."

The queen smiled. "No, it wasn't an accident!" she said in her silvery voice. "Fairy magic made your locket open. I'm afraid we need your help again, girls!"

The two friends turned to stare at each other in surprise, their eyes wide.

"Is it Jack Frost again?" Kirsty asked.

"We'll tell you all about it," replied the queen. "But first . . ." She waved her wand at Rachel's locket. It filled with fairy dust again and swung shut.

"Now," the king said, turning to the fairies. "Where is Holly the Christmas Fairy?"

Kirsty and Rachel watched eagerly as Holly came forward. They had never met the Christmas Fairy before! She had long dark hair, and she wore a red dress that was exactly the same color as a holly berry. Her dress had a hood with fuzzy white trim. Even though Holly was the Christmas Fairy, she looked awfully sad.

"Holly is in charge of putting the sparkle into Christmas," Queen Titania explained.

"That's right," Holly said, sighing. "I organize Santa's elves, and I teach the reindeer to fly. It's my job to make sure that Christmas is as sparkly and happy as possible."

"But this year, Jack Frost is causing trouble," the king told them. "He had said he was sorry for everything he had done and promised to behave."

"But now he is up to his old tricks again," said Queen Titania.

"What happened?" Rachel asked.

"Well, Jack Frost sent a letter to Santa Claus asking for presents," the king went on. "But he got a letter back! It said that he'd been so naughty, he wouldn't be getting any presents at all this year!"

"We'll show you what Jack Frost did next," said the queen. She waved her wand over a small pool of blue water on the ground. The water bubbled and fizzed, and then became smooth as glass.

Pictures appeared on the surface. Kirsty and Rachel could see a big log cabin at night. It was surrounded by deep snow, and icicles hung from the wooden roof. The cabin was full of toys! There were dolls, puzzles, bikes, games, and books

all lying around in huge piles. Kirsty and Rachel had never seen so many toys.

"Oh!" Kirsty gasped. Her hand flew to her mouth. "Rachel, look!"

In the corner of the cabin stood a beautiful wooden rocking horse. Someone was painting gold patterns onto the rockers. He was dressed in red and white, and had a jolly face with a long white beard.

"It's Santa Claus!" Rachel cried happily.

Then the picture changed to show the outside of the cabin again. There the girls could see Santa's sleigh. It was silver and white, and sparkled with magic. Eight reindeer were harnessed to the sleigh. They were waiting patiently, shaking their antlers every so often.

Lots of little elves wearing bright green scurried around the sleigh, filling it with presents. The bells on the tips of their hats tinkled merrily as they rushed back and forth with armfuls of presents.

Kirsty and Rachel were so excited, they almost forgot why they were watching. But then, just as the sleigh was full with presents, Jack Frost appeared.

As Kirsty and Rachel watched, Jack Frost peeked out from behind the log cabin. When the elves had left the sleigh, he ran over to it and jumped in. Grabbing the reins, he shouted a spell to make the reindeer obey him. And then, the sleigh lifted off the ground and zoomed into the starry night sky.

As soon as the elves saw
what was happening,
they chased Jack
Frost. But the magic
sleigh was too fast for
them to catch.

"Oh, no!" Kirsty cried.
"He stole Santa's sleigh!"

"So now you see why we need your
help," said Queen Titania as the pictures
faded away. "Holly has to find Santa's
sleigh and return it before Christmas Eve.
Otherwise, Christmas will be ruined for
all the children around the world!"

"We think Jack Frost has taken the
sleigh to your world," Holly added.
"He loves parties, so he won't want to
miss Christmas. Will you help me track
him down?"

"Of course we will," Rachel and Kirsty replied together.

Holly smiled. "Thank you!" she cried, giving both girls a hug.

"Where should we start?" asked Rachel.

"Like usual, the magic will come to you," the queen said with a smile. "You will know when you are on the right track. And Holly will help. But there is one more thing you need to know…" The queen waved her wand over the pool again. The girls watched as an image of three presents appeared in the water.

They were wrapped in beautiful golden paper and tied with big bows that glittered in all the colors of the rainbow.

"These three presents were on the sleigh when Jack Frost took it. They are very special," the queen explained. "Please try to find them all."

"We'll do our best," said Kirsty, while Rachel nodded.

The king stepped forward, holding a golden bag. "This will help you defeat Jack Frost," he said. He opened the bag and showed the girls a sparkling fairy

crown. "It has powerful
magic. If Jack Frost
puts it on his head,
he will immediately
be brought here,
where he will appear
before me and Queen Titania."

Kirsty took the bag and put the strap
over her shoulder.

"Good luck, Rachel and Kirsty!" called
the queen. She raised her wand and sent
another shower of fairy dust whirling
and swirling around the girls. Rachel and
Kirsty were lifted off their feet to begin
the journey home.

BUTTONS ON THE LOOSE!

"We're back!" Rachel said as the sparkling clouds of fairy dust cleared. The girls were in the Walkers' garage again.

"And we're back to normal size," Kirsty added, brushing a speck of fairy dust from her jeans. "Poor Holly. I hope we can help her."

"We'll find Jack Frost!" said Rachel.
"But we'd better take these Christmas
decorations inside now. Mom will
wonder where we've been."

Kirsty dropped the tiny golden bag into
her pocket for safekeeping. Then she
helped Rachel carry the boxes into the
house. Once the girls were inside, they
started looking through the decorations.

"I see what you mean about this star," Kirsty said, holding up a big, tattered silver star.

"Maybe Mom will let me buy something new for the top of the tree," replied Rachel. "I'd love to have a fairy this year!"

The girls spent the rest of the afternoon sorting through the decorations. Rachel's dad got home from work at six o'clock, and then they all went to Hillfield's Farm to pick out a Christmas tree.

"It looks like everyone else had the same idea!" Rachel's mom said as the car pulled up outside the farm. Lots of people were looking at Christmas trees.

There seemed to be hundreds of trees in all shapes and sizes.

"At least there are plenty of trees!" Kirsty laughed.

"And we'll find the perfect one," Rachel added, climbing out of the car.

The two girls hurried across the parking lot, Mr. and Mrs. Walker followed with Buttons. The evening was cold and clear, and stars glittered in the dark sky.

"Don't pick one that's too big," called
Mrs. Walker. "We'll never get it through
the front door."

Rachel and Kirsty wandered
up and down the rows of
trees. But they couldn't
seem to find one that
was just right. They
were all too big,
too small, too bushy,
or too skinny.

Then Rachel's eyes
fell on a tree up ahead.
The needles were so
green and shiny, they
almost seemed to glow in
the frosty air. *That tree looks perfect*, she
thought, as she went over to it. *It's not too
big and it's not too small.*

Suddenly, Rachel spotted a bright red glow, right in the middle of the tree. Then a tiny face peeked out at her.

"It's me!" Holly cried, waving her wand and sending little sparkly red holly berries bouncing around the tree branches.

Rachel laughed. "Kirsty, over here!" she called.

Kirsty rushed over. "What are you doing here, Holly?" she asked. "Is Jack Frost nearby?"

But before Holly could answer, there
was a shout from Mrs. Walker. Buttons ran
past the girls, his leash trailing along behind
him. He was barking loudly.

"Stop him, girls!" cried Mrs. Walker.
"I don't know what's wrong with him. He
pulled the leash right out of my hand."

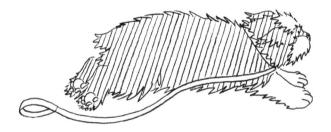

"We'll catch him, Mom," Rachel called.
"Keep an eye on our tree."

Holly hopped inside Kirsty's pocket, and
then the girls ran after the excited dog.
Buttons had left the farmyard and was
racing toward an oak tree. Suddenly, Kirsty

saw a shadow jump
out from behind the
tree and head for
an old barn. Even
though it was dark,
she could just make
out a pointed nose
and big feet.

"Oh!" she gasped,
"I think Buttons is
chasing one of Jack
Frost's goblins!"

"I knew they were
around here somewhere!" Holly cried.
"Quick! After him!"

Buttons was standing outside
the barn, sniffing at the door.

"The goblin must be inside," Rachel
whispered, grabbing the dog's leash.

Quickly, she hooked it
over a nail in the barn
wall, and gave Buttons
a pat. "Wait here,
Buttons," she whispered.
"We won't be long."

"Let's look inside,"
Kirsty suggested. She
pulled the barn door open and they all
peeked in. A cold blast of icy air swirled
around them. The girls and Holly could
see across the barn to the big doors on
the opposite side. Those doors were wide
open, and a sparkling trail led out of the
barn and up into the sky. They could
make out a glittering silver shape traveling
very fast. It was Santa's missing sleigh!

GRUMPY GOBLINS

"Jack Frost was here," Kirsty said, looking disappointed. "We just missed him!"

"That must be why it's so cold," Holly agreed with a shiver.

The barn was full of bales of straw. Looking around, Rachel noticed that there was wrapping paper scattered all over them. "Jack Frost has been opening Santa's presents!" she said. "He's the worst!"

"Shh!" Holly whispered. "Goblins!"

Two goblins had just rolled out from behind one of the straw bales. They were fighting and yelling at each other.

"It's mine!" shouted one goblin with a wart on his nose.

"No, it's mine!" yelled the other.

"Look," Rachel said. She pointed at the present the goblins were arguing over. "It's one of the three special presents that the queen asked us to look for!"

"We have to get that present," said Holly.

"The other two presents must still be on

the sleigh," Kirsty added. "I don't see any more of that special gold wrapping paper anywhere."

The goblins were still fighting, rolling around on the floor of the barn.

"Give it to me!" yelled the warty one. "There might be Christmas cookies inside, or fruitcake, or—"

The other goblin licked his lips. "I'm going to eat them all!"

"What are we going to do?" Rachel whispered. "How are we going to get the present back?"

Kirsty frowned. "I have an idea," she said. "That goblin seems to like Christmas cookies. Holly, could you use your magic to make it smell like cookies?" Holly's eyes twinkled. "Of course," she replied.

"We'll tell the goblins there's a big plate of cookies in the hayloft," Kirsty continued. "They're so greedy, they'll go and look. And they can't climb the ladder and hang on to the present at the same time. We'll be able to grab it!"

Rachel and Holly beamed at her.

"Great idea!" said Holly. "One magic Christmas cookie smell coming up!" She flew toward the goblins.

HOLLY'S MAGIC TRICK

Rachel and Kirsty watched anxiously as Holly fluttered over the goblins' heads. They were so busy fighting, they didn't notice her.

Holly waved her wand in the air. A few seconds later, the smell of freshly-baked cookies wafted around the barn. Even Rachel and Kirsty, who were standing outside, could smell it.

The goblins stopped fighting. They lifted their big noses into the air and sniffed.

"Fresh cookies!" Holly called, pointing at the ladder to the hayloft. "Up in the hayloft. Help yourselves!"

"Cookies! Yum!" shouted one of the goblins. He tossed the present to the other one and ran for the ladder. But the other goblin didn't want to be left behind. He raced over to the ladder too. As soon

as he realized that he
couldn't climb up to
the loft with the
present in his arms,
he threw it down
on a pile of straw.

Rachel and
Kirsty laughed,
as they watched
the goblins
scrambling up
the ladder, trying
to push each
other out of the
way. Once they
had reached the
top, the girls ran
into the barn. Kirsty
picked up the present.

Suddenly, there was a shout from above. "There aren't any cookies here! We've been tricked!"

One of the goblins peered down into the barn. "Where's that Christmas fairy?" he yelled.

"Quick!" Holly gasped. "Let's get out of here!"

The girls and Holly ran for the door as the goblins tumbled down the ladder. "After them!" the first goblin shouted.

54

Outside of the barn, Rachel fumbled to free Buttons' leash from the nail. The goblins appeared in the doorway and ran toward her. But Buttons began to bark loudly as soon as he saw them. The goblins looked frightened.

"*You* get the present back!" the first goblin yelled, nudging the other.

"No, *you* get it!" his friend shouted.

Still barking, Buttons began pulling Rachel toward the goblins. Immediately, the two terrified goblins sprinted back into the barn and shut the door.

"Good dog!" said Rachel, patting Buttons to calm him down. At the same time, Kirsty showed the present to Holly.

"Hooray! We've found one special present," Holly beamed. "I'll get this back to Fairyland right away." She waved her wand over the gift. The present disappeared in a magic cloud of sparkling red holly berries.

"We'll see you again soon," Rachel called, as Holly fluttered up into the sky.

"I'll be back as soon as I find out where Jack Frost is!" Holly promised.

Rachel and Kirsty hurried back to the farmyard to find Mr. and Mrs. Walker. They had bought the tree Rachel had picked out, and were tying it to the roof of the car.

"Now, I think it's time we all went home and had some Christmas cookies and hot chocolate," said Rachel's mom as they climbed into the car.

Rachel and Kirsty grinned at each other.

"Cookies would be great, Mom," said Rachel, trying not to laugh.

"I think Buttons deserves a cookie too," Kirsty whispered. "After all, he was the one who led us to the goblins and the first present."

Woof! Buttons agreed.

"Yes, and our fairy adventures aren't over yet," Rachel whispered back, her eyes shining. "We'll save the sleigh. This is going to be the best Christmas ever!"

BOOK TWO

A NARROW ESCAPE
TABLE OF CONTENTS

CHRISTMAS SHOPPING

"Two days until Christmas!" Rachel said the next morning. She stood in front of the bedroom mirror, brushing her hair. The girls were getting ready to go Christmas shopping with Rachel's mom. "Isn't it exciting, Kirsty?"

Kirsty nodded. "I can't wait!" she said. "But I don't want it to get here *too* soon.

We have to find Jack Frost
and Santa's sleigh first."

"I know," Rachel agreed.
"Once we're done helping
our fairy friends, we can really
enjoy Christmas."

"I need to buy a present for my
mom," Kirsty said. "Do you have
many presents left to buy?"

Rachel shook her head. "Only
one," she replied.

"But the mall has
great Christmas
displays, so it's fun
to look around
even if you don't
have much shopping to do."

"Girls, are you ready yet?"
Mrs. Walker called up the stairs.

"Coming, Mom," Rachel yelled back.

The girls ran downstairs, laughing and chatting. Mrs. Walker was waiting for them in the hall. "Don't forget your scarves and mittens," she said, picking up her car keys. "It's freezing today, and the mall parking lot is big. We may have to walk a little after we park the car." She opened the front door and went to get the car out of the garage.

A blast of cold air swept through the open door. It rustled through the tinsel on the Christmas tree. "Brr!" Rachel gasped, grabbing her coat. "Mom's right. It *is* cold today."

"Doesn't the tree look pretty?" asked Kirsty, pulling on her mittens. The Walkers had a big entrance hall, and they had put the tree

in a corner near the stairs. Rachel and Kirsty had decorated it, and now it glittered and gleamed with ornaments, tinsel, and garland.

"It's the nicest one we've ever had," Rachel agreed. "But I'll unplug the lights now, since we're going out."

Kirsty watched as Rachel unplugged the Christmas tree lights. Then she noticed that something was different about the tree. Instead of the tattered silver star she had placed on the top, there now sat a beautiful, sparkly fairy!

Kirsty stared in surprise and she realized that it was a *real* fairy.

Holly was perched on top of the tree, glowing brightly, and waving at Kirsty!

"Holly!" Kirsty laughed. "What are you doing up there?"

"I thought your tree was missing a fairy!" Holly grinned.

Rachel looked up in time to see Holly fly down and land on Kirsty's shoulder. "Hello, Rachel," Holly sang. "I have a feeling something magical is going to happen today! Can I come to the mall with you?"

"Of course," Rachel replied happily. "But you'll have to hide from my mom!"

"No problem," Holly winked at the girls and snuggled down inside Kirsty's coat pocket, folding her wings neatly. She popped out a second later and said "Don't forget the magic crown!"

"It's in my pocket," Rachel assured her.

Just then, they heard Rachel's mom honk the car horn.

"I hope something magical happens today!" Rachel whispered to Kirsty as they rushed outside. "Maybe today we'll get Santa's sleigh and the two special presents back."

"I hope so!" Kirsty agreed with a smile.

A Chilling Suspicion

Even though it was still early in the morning, the mall was already crowded when they arrived. Mrs. Walker drove around the parking lot, and it took them a while to find an empty parking space.

"Now, Rachel," she said as they all climbed out of the car, "would you and Kirsty like to go shopping on your own?

I have to buy some presents that I don't want you to see!"

"Like what?" Rachel asked curiously.

Her mom laughed. "If I tell you, then they won't be a surprise, will they?" she said. "We'll split up, and I'll meet you and Kirsty in an hour by the elevators. Make sure you stay inside the mall and stay together."

"OK," the girls agreed.

Mrs. Walker went up the elevator, while the girls stayed on the first floor. They walked around the mall, looking at the Christmas displays in the store windows.

Christmas songs were playing over the speaker system, and people were rushing all around, carrying lots of shopping bags.

Before long, Rachel and Kirsty had finished their Christmas shopping. Kirsty bought some pretty silver earrings for her mom, and Rachel bought a book for her dad.

"Are you OK in there, Holly?" Kirsty whispered, putting the earrings into her other pocket.

Holly nodded. She was peeking out of Kirsty's pocket to see what was going on. She was so small, nobody noticed her among the hustle and bustle.

"Let's go see the Christmas display," Rachel said to Kirsty. "It's beautiful!"

Kirsty nodded eagerly, and Rachel led the way to the big central area of the mall. There, right in front of them, was Santa's Workshop.

"Wow!" said Kirsty, her eyes wide. "This is fantastic!"

The workshop was a huge white tent covered in sparkling lights. They changed color from white to blue to silver, and then back again. Long, glittering icicles hung from the roof. The tent was surrounded by fake snow, and there were huge toy polar bears and penguins that waved at the shoppers. Next to the tent, there was a small ice rink. Boys and girls dressed as elves were skating back and forth. Some carried brightly wrapped packages, while others performed spins and jumps.

A little bridge made of sparkling icicles led the way into the tent.

"Isn't it pretty?" Rachel asked, as they moved closer to get a better look.

There was a long line of children waiting to see Santa. Rachel and Kirsty were standing near the bridge, watching the elves on the ice rink, when a little girl ran out of the tent to join her mom. She seemed upset! Kirsty and Rachel couldn't help overhearing what she said.

"Did you have a good time, honey?" the mother asked.

"Well, Santa's sleigh was all sparkly," the little girl told her breathlessly, "and his reindeer were furry and friendly. But Santa wasn't very nice!" She stuck her bottom lip out as if she was about to cry. "He wouldn't let me have a present, even though he had lots and lots of them. And he was all cold and spiky!"

Immediately, Rachel's ears pricked up. That didn't sound like Santa at all. But it did sound like someone else she knew— someone mean and tricky. They might just have found Jack Frost!

NOT THE REAL SANTA!

"Kirsty!" Rachel said, pulling her friend to one side. She didn't want their conversation to be overheard. "Did you and Holly hear that? I think Jack Frost might be inside the tent, pretending to be Santa!"

Kirsty stared at Rachel. "You could be right!" she gasped.

"Yes," Holly piped up. "We'd better check it out."

"How are we going to get into the tent?" asked Rachel. "It'll take forever if we have to wait in line."

"She's right," Kirsty said. "Let's try to slip in the back and see what's going on."

 The girls crept around the back of the tent, keeping an eye out for anyone who might try to stop them. But they found the tent was tied down so firmly, they couldn't sneak underneath.

"Leave it to me!" Holly
whispered. She waved her
wand, and a shower
of sparkling red fairy
dust fell onto one
corner of the tent.
Immediately, the
ropes loosened,
and part of
the canvas
curled upward.

"Thanks, Holly!"
said Rachel. "Come
on, Kirsty."

The two girls crept cautiously under
the edge of the tent. Inside, there were
lots of glittering ice-covered rocks.
Rachel, Kirsty, and Holly hid behind
them while they looked around.

The tent was lit with rainbow-colored
lanterns that glowed brightly. Long,
gleaming icicles hung from the ceiling,
and a big Christmas tree stood in one
corner. It was decorated with shiny silver
balls and multicolored fairy lights.

Kirsty shivered. The air inside the tent
felt frosty. "It's really cold in here," she
whispered. "Jack Frost must be nearby."

And, sure enough, in the middle of the room was Santa's sparkling sleigh, complete with hundreds of presents, eight magical reindeer, and Jack Frost! He was ripping open a present. The ground in front of him was already covered with wads of wrapping paper. He wore a red Santa suit and a fake white beard. But he still looked like his mean, cold self.

"Bring me another present!" he roared, tossing aside the board game he'd just opened.

The goblins came rushing from every corner of the tent. They were all carrying presents, which they pushed into Jack Frost's greedy hands. Rachel and Kirsty held their breath nervously as goblins hurried past their hiding place.

Suddenly, Kirsty spotted something.
"Look!" she hissed, pointing at the
sleigh. "It's one of the
special presents!"
The shiny,
gold-wrapped
package was
sitting at the
back of the sleigh,
on top of a pile of
other presents.

"You're right," Holly whispered
excitedly. "And the third one must still
be on the sleigh somewhere, too. It
doesn't look like Jack Frost has opened
it yet."

"But how are we going to get to them
without Jack Frost and his goblins seeing
us?" Rachel asked.

"If we stay behind the rocks, we can crawl around to the back of the sleigh without being seen," said Kirsty.

"And I can help you," Holly added eagerly. "I'll distract Jack Frost and the goblins."

"How?" asked Kirsty.

"I'll use magic to put myself inside one of the presents that Jack Frost is opening," Holly replied.

"That will give him a surprise!"

"That's a great idea," Rachel declared. "We'll creep around to the back of the sleigh. Then, while Holly creates a diversion, you grab the present, Kirsty. I'll try to drop the magic crown on Jack Frost's head."

"OK. Let's go," Kirsty whispered.

Holly nodded. She waved her wand above her head and immediately disappeared.

Rachel and Kirsty began to crawl on their hands and knees toward the sleigh, staying out of sight behind the rocks. Jack Frost was too busy unwrapping presents to notice them.

And, luckily, the goblins were running backward and forward, trying to keep Jack Frost happy.

Their hearts thumping, the girls got closer and closer to the sleigh. The special present was so close now that Kirsty could reach out and touch it.

"Now we just wait for Holly to make her move," Rachel whispered.

The girls watched Jack Frost tear the paper off another present. "I'm bored," he grumbled. "Why can't I get a really nice present?" He threw the wrapping paper on the floor and held up a pretty wooden box. "I wonder what's inside?" he muttered.

Suddenly, the lid of the box burst open. Holly shot out in a huge shower of glittering red holly berries and fairy dust. Jack Frost and the goblins coughed and spluttered in shock.

"This is our chance!" Kirsty cried, as Jack Frost and his goblins stared at Holly in surprise.

THE CHASE IS ON!

Kirsty reached for the special present.
Meanwhile, Rachel pulled the crown out
of her pocket and stood up, ready to drop it
onto Jack Frost's head.

"What's going on?" Jack Frost shouted,
rubbing fairy dust out of his eyes. "It's that
pesky Christmas Fairy, isn't it? Grab her!"

Kirsty had her hands on the present now, and Rachel was leaning over the sleigh with the crown. But just then, one of the goblins spotted her. "Look out!" he screeched, pointing a bony finger at Rachel.

Jack Frost spun around. His cold, hard eyes met Rachel's, and she felt herself shiver. Quickly, Jack Frost waved his wand. The reindeer galloped off, pulling the sleigh behind them. Luckily, Kirsty was still hanging onto the ribbon that was tied around the special package.

As the sleigh started to move,
the present tumbled off the
back and fell safely into
Kirsty's arms.

"I want you to catch
that fairy!" Jack Frost
roared at the goblins
as the reindeer
galloped toward
the tent entrance,
taking the sleigh
with them. "And
those girls, too!"

"Kirsty! Rachel!"
shouted Holly, who
was zooming up and
away from the goblins.
"You have to get out
of here!"

The reindeer galloped out of the tent
and flew up into the air. As the sleigh
soared overhead, the shoppers looked
up in amazement. They gasped, and
then began clapping and cheering,
thinking it was some sort of Christmas
magic show.

The sleigh flew through the mall and out the big double doors. But back in the tent, the goblins were closing in on the girls, backing them into a corner. "We've got you now!" one of them snarled.

"You can't trick us and get away with it!" sneered another.

Kirsty and Rachel were very scared. "Split up and run for it, when I give the word!" Rachel whispered. She waited until the goblins were close to them, and then shouted, "Now!"

Immediately, she and Kirsty ran as fast as they could in opposite directions. The goblins chased after them, but there was a lot of pushing and shoving and shouting. The clumsy goblins bumped into one another and tripped over their own big feet!

In the middle of the chaos, Rachel and Kirsty both headed for the exit. Kirsty reached it first. She noticed that Rachel was almost there, too, but a goblin was very close behind her. As Kirsty slipped out of the tent, she saw the goblin reach for her friend!

THE GREAT ESCAPE!

The goblin missed Rachel and fell over, tripping another goblin who was hot on his heels. The girls had escaped from the tent, but they knew that the goblins were right behind them. They didn't have much time.

"Quick, Kirsty!" Rachel shouted. "Those ropes that hold up the back of the tent—we need to pull them out!"

Kirsty knew exactly what Rachel
had in mind. The two girls began
pulling the ropes with all their might.

Suddenly, there was a creaking sound
as the ropes gave way. The large white
tent wobbled and fell to the ground,
trapping the goblins underneath the
heavy canvas.

"We did it!" Kirsty gasped. "That was
a great idea, Rachel!"

"Yes, but I think we'd better get out of here before those goblins escape," Rachel whispered. "It's almost time to meet Mom anyway."

"Where's Holly?" asked Kirsty, looking around.

"Here I am!" called a tiny voice. Holly zoomed over to land on Kirsty's shoulder. All the shoppers were too busy staring at the collapsed tent to notice the tiny fairy.

"Are you all right?" Rachel asked anxiously.

"I'm fine!" Holly beamed.

"Thank you for getting the second present. The Fairy King and Queen will be so happy!"

Kirsty held out the present, and Holly waved her wand over it. Fairy dust filled the air, and the present promptly vanished back to Fairyland.

"I almost got the crown on Jack Frost's head!" Rachel sighed as she dropped the crown carefully back into her pocket. "But he got away again. And we don't know where he went."

"Oh, yes, we do!" Holly told her excitedly. "While you were running from the goblins, I followed the sleigh and spoke to one of my reindeer friends."

"What did he say?" asked Rachel eagerly.

"He told me Jack Frost is really annoyed that we keep finding him in the human world," Holly explained.

"He wants to open all of Santa's presents in peace and quiet. So he told the reindeer to take him to his ice castle right away."

"His ice castle!" Kirsty exclaimed. "Where Jack Frost lives?"

Holly nodded.

"Do you know where it is, Holly?" Rachel asked.

"Yes," Holly replied. "It's a cold, scary place, but I can take you there tomorrow, if you still want to help."

"Of course we do!" said Kirsty and Rachel together.

Holly beamed at them. "I'll head back
to Fairyland now and report to King
Oberon and Queen Titania," she went
on. "Can you get me out
of the mall?"

"Of course,"
Kirsty said, smiling.
While Holly hid
behind Kirsty's
scarf, the girls walked
quickly over to one of the

doors. When nobody was
looking, Holly slipped out
from behind the scarf,
gave the girls a cheery
wave, and zoomed up
into the sky. The girls
watched her fly away
until she was out of sight.

Then they hurried back through the mall toward the elevators, where they had promised to meet Rachel's mom.

Mrs. Walker was already waiting for them, holding lots of shopping bags.

"Hello, girls!" she smiled. "I thought you'd gotten lost! Did you both find everything you needed?"

"Almost!" Rachel replied with a quick glance at Kirsty.

"Did you see Santa's workshop?" Mrs. Walker went

on, leading the way back to the car. "I heard it was beautiful—until the tent collapsed! But some of the parents were complaining that Santa Claus was awfully grumpy."

Rachel and Kirsty grinned at each other. "He was!" Kirsty agreed.

"I wonder what's going to happen tomorrow, Rachel?" Kirsty whispered as Mrs. Walker unlocked the car. "Jack Frost's ice castle sounds scary."

"I know," Rachel whispered back.

"But we can't let our fairy friends down."

"No we can't," Kirsty said firmly. "We have to get Santa's sleigh and the third present."

"And this time, we'll get that magic crown on Jack Frost's head!" added Rachel. The girls exchanged a smile and climbed into the car. The were both very excited and a little bit nervous about what the next day might have in store!

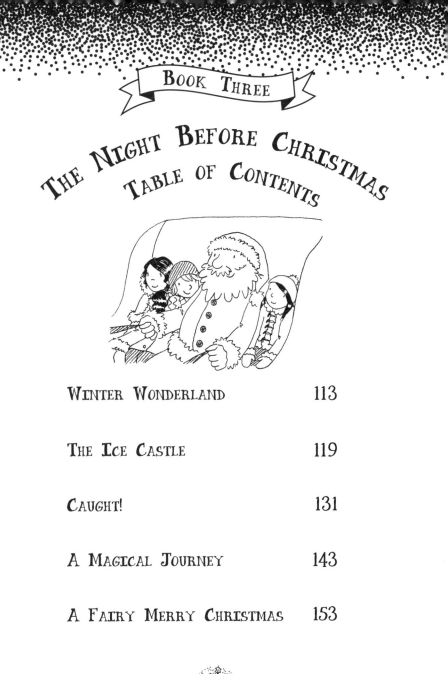

BOOK THREE

THE NIGHT BEFORE CHRISTMAS
TABLE OF CONTENTS

WINTER WONDERLAND

Rachel opened her eyes and yawned. She sat up in bed and looked over at Kirsty, who was still asleep. *It's Christmas Eve!* Rachel thought excitedly. But it would only be a merry Christmas if they managed to get the sleigh and all the presents back to Santa today.

If they didn't, Jack Frost would ruin everything!

Rachel pushed back the blankets and shivered. Even though the heat was on, there was still a chill in the air. She went over to the window and looked outside. "Oh!" she gasped.

It had snowed heavily during the night, and the trees, the grass, and the shrubs were all hidden under a thick blanket of sparkling white snow.

"What is it?" Kirsty yawned.

"Sorry, did I wake you?" asked Rachel.
"I was just so surprised to
see the snow!"

"Snow?" Kirsty
gasped. She jumped
out of bed and
ran over to join
Rachel. They
both peered
out of the
frosty window.

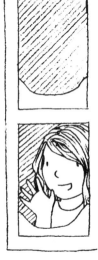

"It looks like
we're going to have
a white Christmas," Rachel smiled.

"It'll be the best Christmas ever," Kirsty
agreed. "As long as we make it back from
Jack Frost's ice castle . . ."

"Are you scared?" asked Rachel.

"A little," Kirsty replied. "But I'm not giving up. Are you?"

"No way!" Rachel laughed. "Come on. Let's get dressed and have breakfast. Then we can go outside."

The two girls hurried downstairs for scrambled eggs and toast. Then they

pulled on their coats and boots, and ran out into the yard. Their feet sank into the soft snow, leaving tracks all over the lawn. It started snowing again, and pretty snowflakes drifted down around them.

Kirsty rolled a
snowball in her hands.
"Let's have a snowball
fight!" She grinned
and threw the snowball
at Rachel.

Laughing, Rachel
ducked. But before the
snowball reached her, it exploded in the
air like fireworks. Tiny sparkling red icicles
shot in all directions. As Kirsty and Rachel
watched in amazement, Holly burst out of
the snowball.

"Here I am!" she cried, shaking
snowflakes from her red dress. "Are you
ready, girls? It's time to go to Jack Frost's
ice castle!"

THE ICE CASTLE

"We're ready!" Rachel said bravely.

Kirsty nodded and checked her coat pocket to make sure she had the magic crown.

Then Holly waved her wand in the air. Berry-red fairy dust drifted down over the girls, and they began to shrink. In a moment, they were fairy-size and had thin wings on their backs.

Holly fluttered up into the air, and Rachel and Kirsty followed her.

"Here we go!" Holly said, waving her wand again.

It was snowing heavily now, and the falling snowflakes began to spin and dance around the girls until Rachel and Kirsty couldn't see anything at all.

Then, the blizzard of snow cleared
as quickly as it had begun. Rachel and
Kirsty gasped. They weren't in the
Walkers' back yard anymore. Instead,
they were sitting in a
tree, staring at Jack
Frost's ice castle.

The castle stood
on a tall hill
under a gloomy,
gray winter sky.
It was built out
of sheets of ice.
It had five towers
tipped with icy
blue peaks. The ice
glittered and sparkled
like diamonds, but the palace
still looked cold and scary.

"Be careful," Holly whispered as a couple of goblins wandered underneath the tree. "There are goblins everywhere. We'll never get in through the main gate."

"Maybe we can find a way in from above," Rachel suggested, looking upward.

"Good idea," Holly replied. "Follow me!"

The girls trailed Holly as she flew up toward one of the ice-blue towers.

"See what I mean?" Holly said quietly.

Rachel and Holly peered down at the castle below.

Holly was right. There were goblin guards at every door!

"Maybe we can find an open window," whispered Rachel.

Holly nodded. "Let's split up and take a look. We'll meet back here in a few minutes."

They all flew off in different directions. Kirsty went to look around the tops of the towers, one by one.

There were lots of windows, but all of them were locked. She flew back to meet Rachel and Holly.

Rachel was already waiting. "I didn't have any luck." She sighed. "Did you?"

Kirsty shook her head sadly.

At that moment, Holly fluttered down to join them.

"Did you get lost?" asked Kirsty.

"I had to hide from one of the goblins," Holly explained. "He was on guard duty, and he almost spotted me!"

"We didn't find any open windows,"
Rachel told her. "Did you?"

Holly shook her head. "No, but I
found another way in!" She grinned.
"Follow me."

Holly led the girls
to a roof on the castle
and pointed down.
"Look!" she said.

"A trap door!"
Kirsty gasped.

"When I was hiding
from the goblin, I
saw him lift the trap
door and go into the
castle," Holly told
them. "And I don't
think he locked it on
the other side."

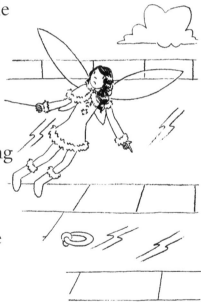

They checked to make sure that there were no goblins around, then flew down to the trap door. It was a slab of ice with a steel ring on the top.

"It looks very heavy," Rachel said with a frown.

"That's no problem," Holly said, smiling. She waved her wand and the trap door suddenly flew open in a whirl of fairy dust.

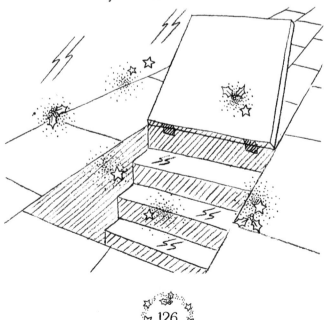

Below were steps
of ice, which led
down into the castle.
Shivering, Rachel,
Kirsty, and Holly
flew inside.

"We have to start
looking for Santa's
sleigh right away,"
Holly whispered to
the girls.

"It's not easy to
hide a sleigh and eight reindeer!"
said Rachel.

"Maybe they're in the stables?"
Kirsty suggested.

"That's a good place to start,"
said Holly. "But keep a look out
for goblins!"

The friends flew down the winding staircase toward the ground floor of the castle. But as they fluttered around a corner, they bumped right into a goblin who was on his way up the stairs.

"Fairies!" the goblin roared. "What are you doing here?" He tried to grab at Holly, but she darted out of reach. "Help! Fairies!"

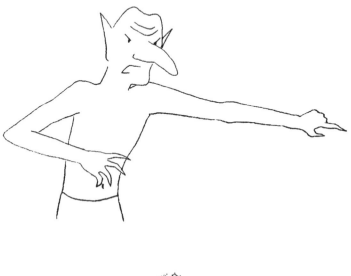

Holly, Rachel, and Kirsty turned and flew back up the stairs. But as they reached the next corner, they heard the loud clatter of footsteps. Six more goblins rushed toward them!

CAUGHT!

The three friends tried to dodge out
of the way, but they were completely
surrounded by goblins. Holly and Rachel
were both caught right away. Kirsty tried
to fly overhead, but one goblin jumped
onto another one's shoulders and grabbed
hold of her ankle.

The goblins laughed gleefully.

"Now you're our prisoners!" they cried. "Jack Frost is going to be so happy with us!"

The goblins took their prisoners through the ice castle and into the great hall. It was a huge room carved from shining sheets of ice. At one end was Jack Frost's throne. It was made of glittering icicles that had been twisted into shape.

But Jack Frost wasn't sitting on his
throne. He was in Santa's sleigh! The
reindeer were still harnessed to it, and
they were munching on bales of hay. Jack
Frost was unwrapping more presents, and
the floor was covered with wrapping paper
and ribbons.

Rachel, Holly, and Kirsty trembled as the
goblins pushed them toward Jack Frost.

"Look what we brought you!" one of the goblins called triumphantly.

Jack Frost looked up at the girls. "You again!" he snarled, staring at them with cold, hard eyes. "You're always trying to ruin my fun!"

He shook his fist. Rachel gasped as she spotted the present Jack Frost was holding in his other hand. He hadn't opened it yet. It was still wrapped in its pretty gold paper and tied with a rainbow-colored bow. It was the third special present that King Oberon and Queen Titania had asked the girls to find!

Rachel glanced at Kirsty and Holly. They'd spotted the present too! But how were they going to keep Jack Frost from opening it?

Kirsty was thinking the same thing as Rachel. She stared down at the piles of wrapping paper on the floor, and suddenly, she had an idea.

"What am I going to do with you?" Jack Frost was muttering, tapping his long, thin fingers on top of the present. "I think I'll put you in my deepest ice dungeon and leave you there for one hundred years!"

"Rachel," Kirsty whispered. "I have an idea. Can you distract the goblins and Jack Frost for a few minutes?"

Rachel looked at her friend curiously, then nodded. "OK," she whispered back.

"Should we take them to the dungeons?" asked one of the goblins.

"I haven't decided yet!" Jack Frost snapped. "Now be quiet while I open this present." He lifted the present and shook it. "I can't wait to see what's inside!"

The goblins moved forward, eager to
see what was inside the package too. The
goblin who was holding onto Rachel
loosened his
grip slightly,
and Rachel saw
her chance. She
zoomed up into
the air, then
flew straight for
the door.

"Get her!"
Jack Frost
yelled furiously.

The goblins
rushed after
Rachel, shouting
and tripping over
one another's feet.

137

At the same time, Kirsty bent down and grabbed a piece of silver wrapping paper and a purple ribbon from the floor. While Jack Frost watched the goblins from the sleigh, Kirsty pulled the gold bag with the magic crown in it out of her pocket. She quickly wrapped it in the silver paper and tied the ribbon around the present. Holly gave her a puzzled look. She had no idea what Kirsty was up to!

Jack Frost was getting angrier and angrier as his goblins tried to catch Rachel. Eventually, he waved his wand, and Rachel's wings instantly froze in midair. She fell to the ground, landing on top of two goblins.

"Now!" Jack Frost snapped as two more goblins dragged Rachel to her feet. "I'm going to open this present!"

"Please, Your Majesty," said Kirsty, stepping forward. "May I say something?"

Jack Frost glared at her. "Make it quick!" he said.

"Won't you take pity on us?" asked
Kirsty. "We only came here to get this
one very special present." She held up
the crown, wrapped in silver paper.
"It's for the Fairy King, and it's very
important. Please let us take it to him!"

Jack Frost's beady eyes lit up as he
stared at the present in Kirsty's hands. "A
present for King Oberon?" he muttered.
"Give it to me!"

"But—" Kirsty began.

"Now!" Jack Frost roared.

A goblin pushed
Kirsty forward.
Jack Frost dropped
the present he was
holding and snatched
the other one out of
Kirsty's hands.

Kirsty tried not to smile. She knew Jack Frost would take the Fairy King's present for himself! Now he was ripping the ribbon and paper away to reveal the golden bag. He put his hand inside and drew out the glittering crown.

"A-ha!" he declared triumphantly. "It's a new crown!" He lifted the crown and lowered it onto his frosty white hair.

Immediately, Jack Frost vanished!

A MAGICAL JOURNEY

The goblins gasped in surprise. They didn't know what had happened to Jack Frost. Would they be next? They ran around the great hall in panic. Some tried to hide under the piles of wrapping paper, while others huddled behind giant icicles.

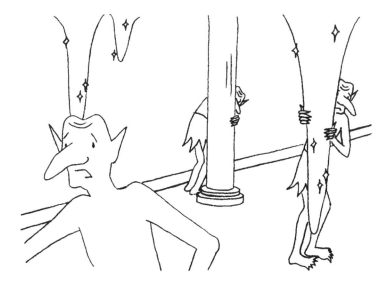

"Great idea, Kirsty!" Holly laughed.

"Jack Frost has been sent to the Fairy King and Queen," cried Rachel. She jumped into the magic sleigh and picked up the third present. "And it's time for us to leave too!"

"But how are we going to get out of the castle?" asked Kirsty as she hopped into the sleigh.

"Don't worry about that," Holly said cheerfully. "The sleigh is magical!" She patted one of the reindeer on the head. "Take us back to Santa, please, my friends!"

The reindeer tossed their antlers joyfully and began to gallop across the great hall. Goblins jumped out of the way as the sleigh picked up speed. Then it rose into the air, heading for the icy roof.

"Oh!" gasped Rachel. "We're going to crash!"

But, magically, the ice melted away as the sleigh approached. Soon the girls were soaring out of the castle and up into the clouds. Then the reindeer raced across the sky so fast that everything was a blur.

"Here's Santa's workshop!" Holly called at last.

The reindeer slowed down, and the sleigh floated toward the ground. Rachel and Kirsty peered out eagerly. Below them, they saw the pretty log cabin

that they remembered from the fairy
pool. And there was a big crowd of elves
outside, dancing in the snow. The bells
on their hats tinkled merrily.

"Hooray!" they cried happily.
"You've found the sleigh
and the reindeer!" As
the sleigh landed, the
elves ran to pet the
reindeer and feed
them carrots.

Rachel and
Kirsty gasped as
Santa himself came
running out of the
cabin. He was in
such a hurry that he
hadn't even buttoned up
his red coat!

"Welcome! Welcome!" Santa called, beaming. "My beautiful sleigh and my precious reindeer are safe, thanks to you!"

"Are we in time to save Christmas, Santa?" Rachel asked anxiously.

Santa nodded. "Oh, yes." He smiled. "It's going to be a wonderful Christmas!"

"But what about the presents Jack Frost already opened?" Kirsty wanted to know.

"Does that mean some children won't get anything?"

"Oh, no!" Santa said, looking shocked. "That would never do! My elves have made plenty of extra presents."

As he spoke, a group of elves ran out of the cabin, carrying armfuls of brightly colored gifts. They piled them up in the magic sleigh.

Santa turned to the girls when the sleigh was full of presents again. "The king and queen will want to see you. Come with me. I'll drop you off on my way to deliver these gifts."

Rachel and Kirsty climbed back into the sleigh. They were going to ride with Santa Claus on Christmas Eve!

Holly joined them as Santa grabbed the reins. "Let's go, my friends!" Santa called happily to the reindeer. "We have a lot of work to do today!"

Rachel and Kirsty grinned at each other as the sleigh rose up into the sky again. They were off to Fairyland!

A FAIRY MERRY CHRISTMAS

As Santa's sleigh got closer to
Fairyland, the girls and Holly could see
sparkling fireworks exploding below
them. The sound of music and fairy
laughter drifted up to the sleigh.

"There's a big party at the palace,"
Holly smiled. "They must have heard
the good news."

The reindeer flew lower, and there was a shout from the fairies below as they spotted the sleigh. Rachel and Kirsty waved as they saw all their old friends waiting for them.

"Wonderful job!" called King Oberon as the sleigh landed.

"You helped Holly save Christmas!"
Queen Titania added.

The fairies cheered as Rachel,
Kirsty, and Holly stepped
out of the sleigh.

"We brought you
this," Rachel said,
handing the third
special present
to King Oberon.

"Thank you!"
The king beamed.
"Will you stay
and join the
party, Santa?"

Santa shook his head.
"I'd love to, but I have a lot
of work to do!" He laughed and shook
the reins. "Merry Christmas!"

"Merry Christmas!" everyone called as the sleigh flew out of sight.

"What happened to Jack Frost?" asked Rachel.

The king frowned. "His magic powers have been taken away from him," he explained.

"And he must stay in his ice castle for a whole year before he is allowed to use magic again!" the queen said. "But now it's time to celebrate Christmas. We have special gifts for all three of you."

She clapped her hands, and two small

fairies hurried forward.
They carried the two
special presents that
Holly had brought back
to Fairyland earlier.

"These presents are
so special because they
are for the three of
you!" the queen said.

Rachel, Holly, and
Kirsty gasped in surprise,
and everyone laughed.

"Since it's Christmas Eve, you can open
them right away." The king smiled and
he handed Holly the package that Rachel
had just given him.

Eagerly, Holly tore the gold paper off
the package, and peeked inside the box.
"A new wand!" she cried. "It's beautiful!"

"It is extra powerful," Queen Titania told her as Holly twirled the wand above her head. It left a trail of magic sparkles behind it and made the sweet sound of tinkling Christmas bells.

"It will help you make Christmas more magical than ever before." The queen smiled.

"Thank you!" Holly beamed.

Queen Titania handed the other two presents to Rachel and Kirsty. They couldn't wait to see what was inside! Rachel

managed to open hers a second before
Kirsty, and she gasped with delight.

"It's a fairy doll!" Rachel said, her eyes
shining. "Look, Kirsty—it's
a fairy for the top of your
Christmas tree!"

The doll sparkled
with magic. She
wore a white dress
that glittered with
silver and gold, and
she had a sparkling
crown over her long
hair. Kirsty had a
doll that was exactly
the same.

"I can't wait to get
home and put it on our Christmas tree!"
Kirsty said, smiling happily.

"There's just one more thing!" The queen laughed. "These dolls are magical. Every year, they will bring you a special Christmas present from the fairies!"

Rachel and Kirsty were thrilled. They'd never expected this!

"But we shouldn't keep you any longer," the king said suddenly. "It's time for you to go home, or you'll be late for Christmas!"

Quickly, the girls said their goodbyes. They both gave Holly a hug, and then the queen waved her wand. "Thank you!" she called. "And Merry Christmas!"

"Merry Christmas!"
Rachel and Kirsty
replied, as they
were caught up in
a whirl of magic
fairy dust.

"Merry
Christmas!"
called all
the fairies.

Suddenly,
the fairy voices
faded away, the
magic dust cleared,
and Rachel and Kirsty
found themselves back to their normal
size in the Walkers' yard.

"We did it, Rachel!" Kirsty laughed
breathlessly. "We saved Christmas!"

"Let's go inside and put my fairy doll on the Christmas tree," Rachel grinned.

The girls ran inside. Kirsty watched as Rachel placed the fairy doll carefully on the top of the tree.

"She looks beautiful!" Rachel said happily.

Just then, the doorbell rang. Rachel ran to see who it was and found Kirsty's mom and dad standing outside.

"Merry Christmas!" said Mr. and Mrs. Tate with a smile.

"Mom! Dad!" Kirsty cried, rushing over to them.

Mr. and Mrs. Tate stayed for hot chocolate and pie, and then it was time for Kirsty to leave. She gave Rachel a big hug.

"Have a great Christmas!" Kirsty told her friend.

"You too," Rachel replied. Then she stood on the doorstep with her mom and dad, waving at the Tates as they drove away.

Mr. and Mrs. Walker closed the front door and returned to the cozy living room, but Rachel stayed in the hall with Buttons. She stared up at the glittering fairy on top of the tree.

Then Rachel blinked hard. Was she seeing things? The fairy had smiled at her, and a cloud of magic sparkles had drifted from her wand!

Rachel looked down to see where the sparkles had fallen—and there was a present under the tree that hadn't been

there before. It was
wrapped in gold
paper and tied with
a bow that glittered
in all the colors of
the rainbow.

Rachel smiled
and patted Buttons.
This really was
going to be the best
Christmas ever!

Did you find all nine letters hidden
throughout the book? The special
holiday word is **Christmas**!

Now it's time for Kirsty and
Rachel to help . . .

EMMA THE EASTER FAIRY.

Read on for a sneak peek . . .

EMMA
THE EASTER FAIRY

A Melted Mess!

"We're finally here!" Rachel Walker cried as her dad pulled the car to a stop in the driveway.

Rachel's best friend, Kirsty Tate, ran across the lawn to say hello.

"We have so many fun things planned," Kirsty said. "We're going to dye eggs for the big Easter egg hunt, and go to Strawberry Farm, and—"

"First we have to unpack," Mrs. Walker

said as Rachel got out of the car. "Rachel, why don't you and Kirsty grab the cooler?"

Rachel and Kirsty each took a handle of the blue cooler and carried it toward Kirsty's house.

"I'm so glad your Aunt Sally lives near Wetherbury," Kirsty said.

"Me, too," agreed Rachel. "We'll have Easter dinner with Aunt Sally, but first we get to spend two whole days with you!" The two girls had met on vacation at Rainspell Island. They were always excited to have a chance to visit each other.

They carried the cooler up the steps to Kirsty's front door.

"This is heavy!" Kirsty remarked. "What's in it?"

Rachel grinned. "It's a special surprise."

When they entered the kitchen, Rachel's parents were talking with Mr. and Mrs. Tate.

"Good to see you, Rachel," said Kirsty's mom.

"What are you carrying in that cooler?"

"Can I tell them, Mom?" Rachel asked.

Mrs. Walker nodded, smiling.

"Mom and I made special Easter chocolates," Rachel said. "There are bunnies, flowers, chicks, and even chocolate eggs. We wrapped them in sparkly paper, too! They look so pretty."

Rachel opened the lid to show them.

RAINBOW magic

More Titles to Read

RAINBOW FAIRIES 1-4

RAINBOW FAIRIES 5-7
+ BONUS PET FAIRY #1

☆ ✩ ☆ ☆ ☆ ✩ ☆

BEHIND THE MAGIC

DAISY MEADOWS is a pseudonym for the four writers of the internationally best-selling *Rainbow Magic* series: Narinder Dhami, Sue Bentley, Linda Chapman, and Sue Mongredien. *Rainbow Magic* is the no.1 bestselling series for children ages 5 and up with over 40 million copies sold worldwide!

GEORGIE RIPPER was born in London and is a children's book illustrator known for her work on the *Rainbow Magic* series of fairy books. She won the Macmillan Prize for Picture Book Illustration in 2000 with *My Best Friend Bob* and *Little Brown Bushrat*, which she wrote and illustrated.